...AND BETWEEN THESE TWO CONTINENTS IS THE ATLANTIC OCEAN.

World map, 1939 boundaries, courtesy of the National Geographic Society

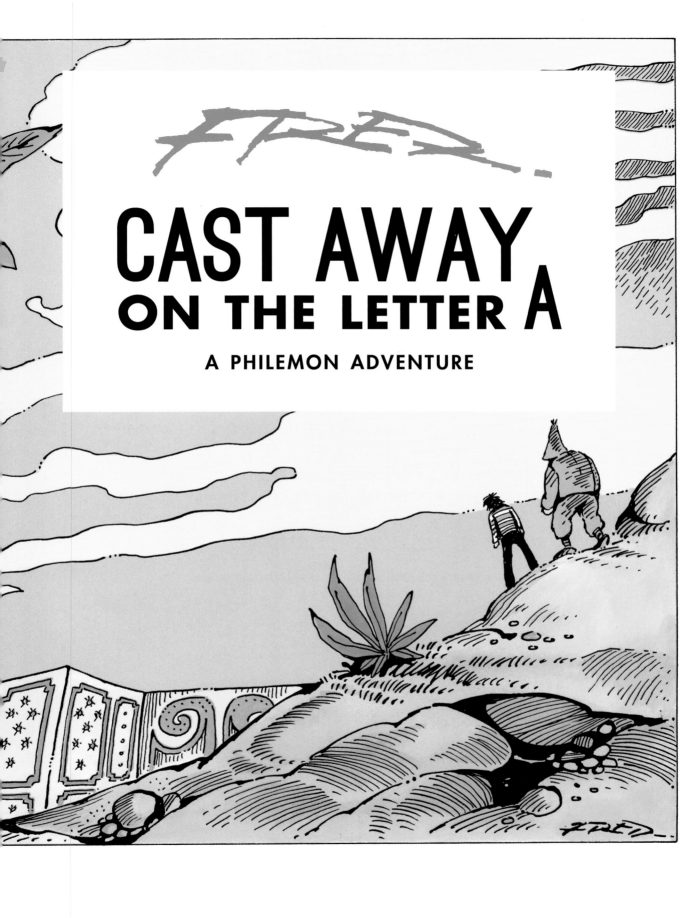

A JUNIOR LIBRARY GUILD SELECTION

Editorial Director: FRANÇOISE MOULY · Book Design: FRANÇOISE MOULY & JONATHAN BENNETT

Translation: RICHARD KUTNER · Hand-lettering: MYKEN BOMBERGER & FRED

FRED'S artwork was drawn in India ink, watercolor and gouache.

ABDOPUBLISHING.COM

Reinforced library bound edition published in 2017 by Spotlight, a division of ABDO, PO Box 398166, Minneapolis, Minnesota 55439. Spotlight produces high-quality reinforced library bound editions for schools and libraries. Published by agreement with TOON Books.

Printed in the United States of America, North Mankato, Minnesota.
042016
092016

THIS BOOK CONTAINS RECYCLED MATERIALS

FOR VISUAL READERS
TOON GRAPHICS

WWW.TOON-BOOKS.COM

LIBRARY OF CONGRESS CATALOGING-IN-PUBLICATION DATA

This book was previously cataloged with the following information:

Fred, 1931- author, illustrator. [Philémon et le naufragé du A. English]
 Cast away on the letter A: a Philemon adventure / by Fred; translated by Richard Kutner.
  pages cm. – (TOON Graphics)
Originally published by Dargaud in 1972 under title: Philémon et le naufragé du A.
Summary: "Young dreamer Philemon lives in the countryside, until one day he falls down a well and finds himself in a parallel world of islands that form the letters of the word Atlantic Ocean. Together with the strange characters he meets there, Philemon must find his way home" – Provided by publisher.
ISBN 978-1-935179-63-4 (hardcover)
1. Graphic novels. [1. Graphic novels. 2. Adventure and adventurers--Fiction. 3. Escapes--Fiction. 4. Islands--Fiction. 5. Alphabet--Fiction.] I. Kutner, Richard, translator. II. Title.
PZ7.7.F73Ph 2014
741.5'944--dc23
                    2013047986

ISBN 978-1-61479-498-1 (reinforced library bound edition)

Spotlight
A Division of ABDO
abdopublishing.com

CAST AWAY
ON THE LETTER A

A PHILEMON ADVENTURE

A TOON GRAPHIC BY

FRED.

MEET PHILEMON

PHILEMON IS AN IMAGINATIVE TEENAGER WHO LIVES ON A FARM IN FRANCE, BACK IN THE 1960S. WHEN A MESSAGE IN A BOTTLE SPARKS HIS CURIOSITY, HE FALLS RIGHT INTO A WORLD OF FANTASTIC ADVENTURES...

ANATOLE IS A DONKEY, PHIL'S TRUSTY FRIEND. HE TRIES TO HELP HIM TO STAY OUT OF TROUBLE, BUT PHILEMON'S ADVENTUROUS SPIRIT AND CURIOSITY GET THE BEST OF HIM.

HECTOR IS PHILEMON'S GROUCHY FATHER, WHO REFUSES TO BELIEVE PHIL'S WILD STORIES.

12

14

A...
A SHARK?

I'M DROWNING...
I NEED AIR... AIR...
AAAAAAH...

WITHOUT AIR, PHIL LOSES CONSCIOUSNESS. SECONDS, MINUTES, HOURS PASS...

OH, MY HEAD...

?

WHAT'S HAPPENING?
AM I ON A BEACH?

THAT'S IMPOSSIBLE!
A BEACH INSIDE A WELL?!
BUT I'M NOT DREAMING.
IT'S REAL SAND!

HEY!

TWO SHADOWS!
HOW CAN I HAVE
TWO SHADOWS?!

18

BUT WHERE DO YOU FIND THE BOTTLES TO SEND YOUR MESSAGES?

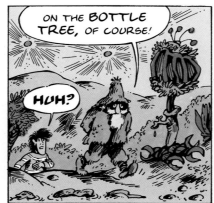

ON THE **BOTTLE TREE**, OF COURSE!

HUH?

YOU MEAN THAT BOTTLES GROW ON TREES?

WELL, **YES**! WHEN THEY'RE RIPE, THEY FALL FROM THE TREES. A LOT OF THEM BREAK, BUT NO BIG DEAL—THERE'S NO REFUND ANYWAY.

BUT THAT'S **IMPOSSIBLE**!

NO, IT'S **NOT** IMPOSSIBLE. BOTTLES ARE **FRAGILE**!

BESIDES, LOOK—HERE'S A BOTTLE TREE NOW.

WATCH YOUR FEET. GLASS IS SHARP.

GOOD GRIEF! BUT... BUT...

BUT **WHERE** ARE WE, ANYWAY?

ON THE "**A**," MY BOY. WE'RE ON THE "**A**"...

THE "**A**"?

YES, THE "**A**"! IT TOOK ME YEARS TO UNDERSTAND.

YEARS, YEARS, YEARS—ONE CAN'T SAY IT DIDN'T TAKE YEARS, YEARS, YEARS...

BUT NOW I'M **SURE**, BECAUSE I SAW THE "**T**," AND I KNOW THAT FARTHER OFF IS THE "**L**"....

WHAT'S HE TALKING ABOUT? HE'S OFF HIS ROCKER! TOO MANY YEARS LIVING ALONE, NO DOUBT...

DINNER IS SERVED!

YES! YUM, YUM! FOLLOW ME, IT'S TIME TO EAT, HA HA!

I'M DYING OF HUNGER. WHAT ABOUT YOU?

?

OH, YES, I FORGOT TO INTRODUCE YOU TO MY BUTLER, FRIDAY.

BAH!

UM... PLEASED TO MEET YOU.

ABOUT TWENTY YEARS AGO, I REMOVED A THORN FROM THIS CENTAUR'S HOOF, AND SINCE THEN HE HAS SERVED ME LOYALLY. HE'S BAD-TEMPERED, BUT HE HAS A KIND HEART.

HMPH!

HA HA!

CLOP CLOP CLOP CLOP

I THOUGHT CENTAURS EXISTED ONLY IN MYTHS.

ME, TOO. MY, OH MY!

DON'T TALK WHEN I'M DRIVING!

THERE ARE LOTS OF CENTAURS ON THIS ISLAND—WILD CENTAURS WHO LIVE IN HERDS.

REALLY?

WE'RE ARRIVING AT MY HUT.

28

WELL, THERE'S GOT TO BE SOME WAY TO LEAVE THIS ISLAND THAT DOESN'T EXIST.

YES, THERE IS A WAY...

...THE WAY THE *UNICORN* TOLD ME.

T-THE *UNICORN*?

YUM! SLURP!

YEP! I CAN GUESS WHAT YOU'RE GOING TO SAY: "A UNICORN? THERE'S NO SUCH THING!" BUT YOU'D BETTER GET IT INTO YOUR HEAD THAT ON AN ISLAND THAT DOESN'T EXIST, **ANYTHING** CAN EXIST!

SO... WHAT'S THE WAY OFF THE ISLAND?

FIRST I NEED TO TELL YOU HOW I MET THE UNICORN—A CHARMING ANIMAL, WELL-MANNERED AND ALL...

PHOOEY!

PLEASE DO.

ABOUT TEN YEARS AGO, AS I WAS DIGGING A WELL ONE DAY—THAT'S MY JOB, WELL DIGGER, YOU UNDERSTAND, AND...

GO ON!

OK! OK! TO MAKE A LONG STORY SHORT, I HEARD A LOUD NOISE BEHIND ME.

BOOM!

?!

A UNICORN HAD FALLEN INTO ONE OF MY WELLS.

HMM...

HMM...

I HELPED IT TO GET OUT, AND TO THANK ME IT SAID:

HE WHO ENTERED BY THE "A" WILL EXIT BY THE "A".

HMM... WHAT DO YOU MEAN BY THAT?

THE LIGHT WILL COME FROM THE SHIPWRECK LAMPS.

AND WHAT DOES **THAT** MEAN?!

31

TCHCRACKK

THE LIGHT WAS COMING FROM THIS DIRECTION. *GOOD GRIEF!* WHERE COULD IT HAVE GONE?

WAIT! THERE'S SOMETHING FLOATING ON THE SEA!

A BOTTLE! **A GIANT BOTTLE!**

CRACK

WHAT'S THAT? IS THERE A SHIP IN IT?

?

CLICK!

CLICK!

THE LIGHTS!

SHEEE

THE PLUG!

CLICK!

THUH! THUH!

PHILEMON, ARE YOU ALL RIGHT?

WAKING ME UP IN THE MIDDLE OF THE NIGHT— UNBELIEVABLE!

?

THUH! THUH!

WHAT'S ALL THIS?

BAH!

THE SHIPWRECK LIGHTS!

I'M GOING TO CATCH A COLD, THAT'S FOR SURE.

SHIPWR—

YES! THEY WERE ATTRACTING A BOTTLE TO CRASH AGAINST THE ROCKS.

A BOTTLE?

A GIANT BOTTLE! AND WITH A SHIP INSIDE!

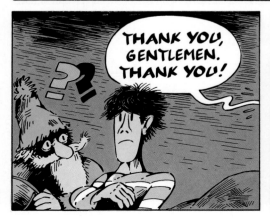

THANK YOU, GENTLEMEN. THANK YOU!

??

CRACK

* THAT'S TRUE!

38

I BET YOU WE HAVEN'T HEARD **THE END** OF THIS STORY. I HAVE A GUT FEELING SOMETHING'S JUST **BEGINNING**!

ABOUT THE AUTHOR

Frédéric Othon Aristidès (1931-2013), known as Fred, is one of France's most influential and revered cartoonists. When he was young, he loved to read Edgar Allan Poe, Charles Dickens, and Oscar Wilde. In the sixties, Fred co-founded *Hara-Kiri*, the leading satirical publication of the May '68 movement–he designed its first 60 covers. Philémon, his story for young readers, was first published in *Pilote* in 1972 by René Goscinny, the author of the Astérix series. Philémon is Fred's most celebrated creation: millions of young French people have grown up with it, and it has inspired many of today's most talented cartoonists. The sixteenth and final volume of Philémon was released in 2013, before Fred's passing. Fred also got to see the beginnings of a Philémon movie, which is currently in the works. While there's no knowing where he found his inspiration, he said he often got his best ideas while taking a bath.

Down the well, in a world of utter fantasy...

As a teenager growing up in Paris in the late sixties, I remember few pleasures–life was mostly a grind of memorization and dull schoolwork. But one day of the week stood out: every Tuesday I'd go out with my dad to the corner newsstand to get a comics magazine, *Pilote*. At the time, I devoured books–I would read as I walked to school and wouldn't even stop to cross the street–but for *Pilote* I slowed down. I took it home and would only look at it while lying down, the door locked. I'd slog through the dull adventure strips first, getting them out of the way so I could get to my favorite humor strips like Astérix or Lucky Luke, and last of all, Fred's adventures of Philémon. I knew that in that first slow, careful reading, and every re-reading after that, I would be rewarded with a wealth of hidden treasures. Fred was a formalist and a deconstructionist, an author who beckoned me, the reader, to enter into the game with him. He lifted the panel borders just enough so you could see the tail of his magician's coat disappear every time you peeked. He opened up a world which has not ceased to delight me ever since. But as quirky and individual as Fred's world is, it is rooted in a deep well of fantasy, a few elements of which we tried to note here.

—FRANÇOISE MOULY, Art Editor, *The New Yorker*

PHILEMON – The name comes from the ancient Greek Φιλήμων, which means only or "best friend". According to the Roman poet Ovid, Philemon and his wife Baucis were a poor, old, and loving couple who lived in Asia Minor and welcomed two strangers into their home when no one else in their town would. The two men turned out to be Zeus and his son Hermes. Zeus led Philemon and Baucis up a hill, where they watched as the god destroyed the town to punish the people for their lack of hospitality (which was considered very important in ancient times). Zeus rewarded Philemon and Baucis for their generosity by making them the guardians of a temple he created where their home stood. When offered a wish, the couple asked Zeus if, when their time came, they could die at the same moment. Zeus granted it: during their last breaths, they were transformed into intertwined trees.

ANATOLE *(page 12)* – Anatole is not the only wise talking donkey. In the Bible, Balaam rides a donkey who goes off the road after it sees an angel barring their path. Balaam beats the donkey before the animal starts talking to him. The donkey explains he has saved his master's life–the angel was there to kill Balaam for his wickedness.

FRIDAY *(page 20)* – Friday is the name of a servant in Daniel Defoe's book *Robinson Crusoe*. In the Philemon story, Friday is a centaur, a creature from Greek mythology with the head and torso of a human and the legs of a horse. Centaurs appear in The Chronicles of Narnia, the Harry Potter series, and in Percy Jackson and the Olympians.

WISHING WELLS *(page 13)* – In Norse mythology, there was a Well of Wisdom, known as Mimir's Well, which would make you wise if you sacrificed something to it. The god Odin threw in his right eye to receive great wisdom. In German and Celtic folklore, wells were believed to grant wishes because gods lived at the bottom of them.

MR. BARTHOLOMEW *(page 21)* – Bartholomew is probably dressed in green because he made his clothes from plants, just like Robinson Crusoe. Leprechauns, a kind of fairy from Irish folklore, also dress in green. They usually look like old men and spend most of their time making shoes. They hide their gold coins in pots at the end of rainbows. If you catch one, he will grant you three wishes in exchange for his freedom.

STRANGE PLANTS *(page 23)* – You'll see a lot of strange plants growing in the pages of this book. You can also find strange plants in the works of Edward Lear, Lewis Carroll, Dr. Seuss, and in *Little Shop of Horrors*. There are also plenty of strange plants in the natural world: the pitcher plant, the Venus flytrap, and the different species of *Rafflesia,* to name a few.

ATLANTIC OCEAN *(page 24)* – The Atlantic Ocean lies between the west coast of North and South America and the east coast of Europe and Africa. The Ancient Greeks believed it was a great river that encircled the world. They called it *Atlantis Thalassa*, which means the "Sea of Atlas." They also called its southern part the "Ethiopic" Ocean, even though it is nowhere near Ethiopia.

RED CARPET *(page 25)* – Red carpets are rolled out for royalty and VIPs (Very Important Persons), such as actors and directors going to the Oscars. In an Ancient Greek play, Agamemnon's angry wife Clytemnestra lays out a red carpet for him when he returns from the Trojan War. Agamemnon knows something is up, because red carpets are reserved for the gods.

BANQUET TABLE *(page 28)* – Banquet tables are at the center of feast halls in Norse mythology. Your rank is indicated by how close you sit to the head of the table–and to the fire. In the Middle Ages, European kings and queens adorned banquet tables with a huge variety of delicious foods in all colors and flavors, served on plates of gold or silver.

UNICORNS *(page 29)* – In ancient times, the unicorn was thought to be a beast with a large, pointed, spiral horn on its head. In European folklore, unicorns were depicted as white horses with such horns. They lived in the woods and were symbols of purity. Belief held that their horn could make unclean water drinkable and heal sickness. You can see a beautiful series of unicorn tapestries at the Cloisters in New York City.

THE SHIPWRECK LIGHTS *(page 32)* – Fred might have gotten his idea for the shipwreck lamps from the will-o'-the-wisp, mysterious lights seen by travelers at night over marshes and swamps. These lights flicker and draw people away from safe paths. They appear mostly in English and European folklore.

DANIEL DEFOE *(page 35)* – Daniel Defoe, an Englishman, is the author of *Robinson Crusoe*, the story of a man shipwrecked on a desert island with his faithful servant, Friday. It is partially based on a true story. In the first 1719 edition, Crusoe is credited as the author, leading many readers of the time to believe that he was a real person.

RAFT OF THE MEDUSA *(page 37)* – In 1816, the French boat *Méduse (Medusa)* ran aground off the coast of present-day Mauritania, in Africa. A raft was constructed and about 150 people crowded on. Only 15 survived the 13 days at sea. The French Romantic painter Théodore Géricault depicted this historical event in a huge, dramatic painting. In Greek mythology, Medusa was a monster with a woman's face and venomous snakes for hair. If you looked at her directly, you turned to stone.

LABYRINTH *(page 40)* – Minos, King of ancient Crete, had a labyrinth, or maze, constructed by the architect Daedalus to hide the Minotaur, a creature half-bull and half-human. No one who entered the labyrinth ever came out–the Minotaur ate them all. Theseus finally put an end to this terrible curse when he killed the Minotaur. The word "labyrinth" can be used to describe any kind of complicated arrangement.

Tips for Parents, Teachers, and Librarians:
TOON GRAPHICS FOR VISUAL READERS

TOON Graphics are comics and visual narratives that bring the text to life in a way that captures young readers' imaginations and makes them want to read on—and read more. When the authors are also artists, they can convey their creative vision with pictures as well as words. They can enhance the overarching theme and present important details that are absorbed by the reader along with the text. Young readers also develop their aesthetic sense when they experience the relationship of text to picture in all its communicative power.

Reading TOON Graphics is a pleasure for all. Beginners and seasoned readers alike will sharpen both their literal and inferential reading skills.

Let the pictures tell the story

The very economy of comic books necessitates the use of a reader's imaginative powers. In comics, the images often imply rather than tell outright. Readers must learn to make connections between events to complete the narrative, helping them build their ability to visualize and to make "mental maps."

A comic book also gives readers a great deal of visual context that can be used to investigate the thinking behind the characters' choices.

Pay attention to the artist's choices

Look carefully at the artwork: it offers a subtext that at first is sensed only on a subliminal level by the reader and encourages rereading. It creates a sense of continuity for the action, and it can tell you about the art, architecture, and clothing of a specific time period. It may present the atmosphere, landscape, and flora and fauna of another time or of another part of the world. TOON Graphics can also present multiple points of view and simultaneous events in a manner not permitted by linear written narration. Facial expressions and body language reveal subtle aspects of characters' personalities beyond what can be expressed by words.

Read and reread!

Readers can compare comic book artists' styles and evaluate how different authors get their point across in different ways. In investigating the author's choices, a young reader begins to gain a sense of how all literary and art forms can be used to convey the author's central ideas.

The world of TOON Graphics and of comic book art is rich and varied. Making meaning out of reading with the aid of visuals may be the best way to become a lifelong reader, one who knows how to read for pleasure and for information—a reader who *loves* to read.

A few nibbles for thought...

• After Philemon asks, "What time is it?" *(page 19)*, a clock appears two panels later. What does this tell you about the place where Philemon has found himself? What expectations do you now have for this story?

• This story is full of comic misunderstandings, as when Philemon and Bartholomew talk about bottles falling from trees *(page 23)*. Identify some of these misunderstandings and explain how they drive the story.

• The unicorn delivers a prophecy *(page 29)*. Why do you think the author chose to include a prophecy in this story? Can you think of other stories involving prophecies, warnings, or coded instructions?

COLLECT THEM ALL!

Set of 6 Hardcover Books ISBN: 978-1-61479-497-4

Hardcover Book ISBN
978-1-61479-498-1

Hardcover Book ISBN
978-1-61479-501-8

Hardcover Book ISBN
978-1-61479-503-2

Hardcover Book ISBN
978-1-61479-499-8

Hardcover Book ISBN
978-1-61479-500-1

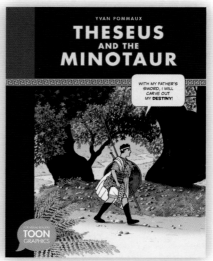

Hardcover Book ISBN
978-1-61479-502-5